JAKE'S SEQUEL

A Sequel to The Woods Within

by

Dr. Milo Yoder Jr.

DORRANCE
PUBLISHING CO
EST. 1920
PITTSBURGH, PENNSYLVANIA 15238

Dorrance Publishing Co
585 Alpha Drive
Pittsburgh, PA 15238
Visit our website at *www.dorrancebookstore.com*

ISBN: 978-1-6853-7387-0
eISBN: 978-1-6853-7531-7

This novel is dedicated to my wife, Judy, and to my son, Erik Yoder, and daughter, Jennifer Johovich, and our three granddaughters, Kensington Swan Rosa Yoder, Jeanne Alyssa Johovich, and Jasmine Ann Johovich.

1

College

When Jake went off to college he was scared. Scared he wasn't smart enough for college level studies, scared to be so far from home, scared to leave his crying Amish mother, and scared his scholarship would not be justified. He also felt a deep loneliness for his girlfriend he left back home. Jake especially missed his terrier, Frisky. This smart little dog was his best friend and confidant for many years. Their relationship wasn't complicated by words that hid other meanings. Several times late at night he cried himself to sleep. He made sure his roommate wouldn't hear him crying. As a little Amish boy, he was told boys don't cry. Once when he was stung by a bee, his older sister Sarah scolded him for being a cry baby. This made a deep mark that stayed with him for the rest of his life. From that time on he never cried in front of anybody.

But his deep well of pent-up curiosity pushed through the wall of scaredness and loneliness. What remained was his profound sadness for the loss of his brother Joe. Joe was a constant measuring stick that lived in his head. Jake also wished he had his brother's brains. He had been told that Joe had an exceptionally high IQ. He took comfort in knowing his brother would be very proud of him being a college student.

In his sadness he struggled with his mother's saying, "Whatever happens is always God's Will". Every time his mother said that he reacted with anger. He would think that would mean that if someone was murdered that would also be God's will. This made no sense to him. Jake could never accept Joe's death as God's will when he died in the car and buggy accident. To him it merely sounded like a stupid circular argument. But he would keep his rage to himself for he was aware how this thinking gave great comfort to his mother. His father, Amos, didn't disclose his thoughts on the matter.

Jake's sadness for his mother was also based on the fact she had been shunned by her family for leaving the Swiss Amish church to join with her husband to the Pennsylvania Dutch Amish. The Swiss Amish were the strictest Amish in America. They disapproved of the Pennsylvania Amish's use of gas engines and having tops on their buggies. The Swiss had to use topless buggies and were only allowed to use straight shafts, not curved, for the horses to pull their buggies.

Shunning meant that while her siblings could occasionally visit, they were forbidden to eat at the same table with his mother. She was shunned most of Jake's entire life, so he knew his mother would never shun him even if he didn't stay Amish. But it was sad to see his mother sorely miss her family and being punished for joining her husband's Pennsylvania Dutch Amish community.

Jake would sometimes find his mother in the living room rocking chair softly crying, tears streaming down her cheeks. It broke Jake's heart to see her so unhappy. When he asked what was wrong, she said she was sad about missing her family and felt bad that they were punishing her with the shunning even though she was a good Amish. Jake was distraught about his inability to comfort her.

At other times she was vivacious, good humored, and loved to sing. Jake often helped her do the evening dishes as they harmonized the familiar Swiss songs and yodels she grew up with. They had to provide their own entertainment since they weren't allowed radios.

In the summertime when Jake and his father were working in the fields his mother would often traipse out to them to bring them fresh homemade lemonade. She was a loving and giving mother and fun to be with except for the times she rocked alone crying after sunset.

But when Jake first entered college, he was inundated both with balled up curiosity and his deep insecurities. His roommate, Bill Stoltzfus, was a tall black-haired basketball player from Pennsylvania who had such an extensive vocabulary it intimidated Jake. He would use words like segue and ubiquitous. He was glad to leave his first language, Swiss German, behind and just concentrate on English. Later at night he would sneak a peek at his dictionary so he wouldn't feel so embarrassed the next day. But Bill was so talkative Jake merely had to interject questions periodically. By the third night he had already learned that Bill was a high school basketball star, an A student and a Presbyterian, although Jake had no clue at the time what that meant.

At the school cafeteria he noticed that Bill appeared careful about what he ate. When asked about that, he explained that he was born with a certain malady where his stomach didn't emit the signals telling him when he was full. That was why he had to mentally decide how much food to put on his plate and stop at that. Otherwise, he would gain far too much weight.

Bill reminded him so much of the "English" kids in high school who were so chatty and full of words. This made it difficult for Jake to discern the deeper meaning that the words covered up.

Jake also really enjoyed his new non-Amish clothes remembering in high school he would change into his Amish clothes immediately after coming home so his mother wouldn't be too upset. He remembered when he was younger his father had bought him and his brother Joe store made light blue shirts with pockets. His mother for some unknown reason didn't remove the pockets to give them a more Amish appearance. Jake loved that shirt. He was glad he no longer had to wear his home-made barn-door pants, shirts and suspenders. Now he wore jeans and a belt and colorful shirts with pockets.

He was especially relieved that he no longer had to attend the Amish Church and engage in the ritual of the Holy Kiss. After joining the Church, the men greet each other with a kiss on the lips that signifies they are now part of the brotherhood. Jake didn't mind this ritual except with one young man who kissed with an open mouth and slobbered all over him. He felt like telling him the kiss wasn't sexual, it was supposed to be a Holy kiss. Jake detested the slobbering kiss and tried to avoid the young man at all costs. He also wondered if the young man might be a closet homosexual.

So, in college he felt he no longer stood out like a sore thumb, but he still never had that feeling that he belonged with the "English" kids in college. While in high school he went to his first barber for a haircut. This created an outcry from the Amish church elders who then came to visit Jake to explain his hair style was simply not acceptable. As a compromise they suggested his should be a little longer and if he needed to part his hair it should be parted in the middle, more like the pictures of Jesus. Jake tried this and because of his narrow head he abhorred the look and never complied. In college he merely continued getting regular haircuts.

One night when Jake came to the dorm late, he realized he interrupted Bill masturbating. Bill merely responded with a chuckle saying, "Well, I guess you caught me in the act." Jake was amazed at the matter-of-factness and complete lack of guilt expressed in Bill's response. Ever since he was twelve years old Jake was wracked with guilt every time the urge overpowered the dictate in his head against this sinful act. He grew up believing that not only was masturbation a sinful act, but even the thought was a sin as the omniscient God could read his thoughts. So, the battle raged on between pleasure and the pain of guilt.

Fear also seemed to be mixed in with the guilt. The fear aspect reminded Jake of the time he was six or seven years old, in the late 1940s, his mother caught him urinating beside the gravel road. She warned him that he shouldn't do that, or big Joe might cut off his looly. The Swiss word for penis.

Big Joe was a huge Black man who was a handyman who worked for Amish families for their wonderful Amish meals. The day he helped Jake's family and ate at their table he made a loud smacking sound while eating. From then on, the family referred to him as "frassy Joe". This Swiss word implied that when Joe ate, he sounded like a pig eating slop. Jake was always scared of "frassy" Joe and was relieved when he no longer came around.

2

Relationships

Caught in between the two cultures, the Amish and the "English", created an unfortunate adaptation for Jake regarding developing relationships. He no longer felt attached to the Amish mindset and he certainly didn't feel like he belonged to the current American culture. His adaptation was that he was neither fish nor fowl so while he outwardly appeared friendly, internally he kept all past and potential relationships at arm's length.

This phenomenon interfered with developing healthy attachments to other human beings. While he felt lonely for his girlfriend back home this feeling was a complicated mixture of missing his Amish mother, his old home, and his whole background.

And besides his girlfriend, Viola, was not an Amish girl. She came from a Mennonite family and at that time Jake couldn't tell the difference between Mennonites and Methodists. They both dressed just like any other American.

One day she came to visit him on the Amish farm in a brand-new Ford automobile. He was somewhat embarrassed for he suspected his mother saw her drive up to the barn where Jake was feeding the horses. He had met her at a school event and was told she was the beauty of the community. She told him that her name was Viola. She surprised him by saying she wanted to be his girlfriend.

Jake suggested they take a walk down the lane that led to the woods. He was totally flummoxed for not knowing what her motivation was behind her statement. Here he was in his Amish clothes, and she wore a pink dress, and her auburn hair framed her beautiful face. He was torn inside thinking three possibilities, what does she want, is she just lying to him, or is she a little stupid.

So, in the lane he started a nasty argument and then realized he hurt her feelings. She responded, "I just thought you were cool, but now you seem sort of mean." Jake apologized for starting an argument and agreed to meet with her again and she became his girlfriend that he missed while in college.

Jake kept his distance from the college girls. They wore tight-fitting colorful sweaters and miniskirts. In his genetics class a dark-haired pretty girl was quite friendly to him. She said her name was Ellen. His quandary was he didn't know where to look. He had to tell himself, don't look at her legs, don't look at her protruding breasts. He didn't know how to read her. Was her underlying message, look but don't touch, or look and touch later? When she asked if she could see him later, he panicked and said no because he had to hit the books. So, he kept his distance.

When he got back to the dorm Bill was there with some guys. Bill said, "Hey Jake, you want to go to the movies with us? We're going to see the new movie, *State Fair*." "Well, ah, ah, I guess so,"

Jake stammered. He wasn't about to disclose that he was absolutely never supposed to go to movies. This would be his first movie. The little Amish boy inside Jake was scared that the judgmental God might strike him dead while he sat in the movie.

By this time a huge gap had developed inside Jake between the scared guilt-ridden boy and the intellectual Jake who couldn't see what could be wrong about going to a movie. The logical side won out. He especially enjoyed listening to Bobby Darin's polished singing voice and was relieved God didn't strike him dead.

3

Sports

Jake loved sports. In high school he had been a star softball pitcher. He had developed a curve ball, a drop ball, and a terrific fast ball. His arms and his wrists were very strong from milking cows by hand. He had set up hay bales in the barn and practiced pitching the twelve-inch softball like his brother Joe had taught him. With practice he learned to pitch underhanded as fast as he could throw overhanded. Since he had to go home right after school hours to do the farm chores, he had to miss some of the team practices. But the coach let Jake come in to pitch the scheduled games.

In college the first scheduled softball game was the freshman team against nine of the younger faculty members. A six-foot-five athlete was the pitcher to start the game who had a good fast ball. Jake didn't know if he could compete with him, but in the fourth inning the coach put him in as the relief pitcher. From then on, he became the starting pitcher.

Jake's biggest regret of this game was that he hit a home run ball, but only made it to third base because he stumbled between first and second base as his cleats caught on the baseline. His brother Joe in his head was severely criticizing him when Ellen from genetics class walked right up to him and said, "You are such a good pitcher. Now that the game is over could we go for a beer?" Jake said he couldn't, that he had a girlfriend back home. "Well in that case I'll leave you alone," she said.

He was so relieved by her response. But the perfectionistic criticalness stayed with him for a long time after the game. That night when he had difficulty going to sleep, he was reminded of the time when his father, Amos, was irritated with him and said, "You're like the East end of a horse going West." This made him chuckle to himself and somewhat eased his criticalness.

Jake also loved to play basketball. But when he was in high school, he was not allowed to try out for the team because he would have to wear basketball shorts which was strictly "verboten" by the Amish besides the fact he wasn't even supposed to be in high school past the age of sixteen.

But in college he wore shorts and played intramural basketball. One day he was surprised when the basketball coach sought him out to ask him to try out for the varsity. Jake was flattered but declined, saying, "Look, I'm only five foot seven. I'd get trounced by all those big guys." The coach replied, "But I've been watching your jump shot. So, think about it."

Jake thought about this but still declined. The real reason was that he was determined to excel in his studies for he knew getting a good education was his ticket out of the Amish culture to a professional work life. If he never had to pitch and haul hog or chicken manure again was just fine by him.

4

Music

Jake loved to sing. His family was a Swiss Amish singing family. They mainly sang Swiss yodeling songs that had been handed down from the Alsace-Lorraine region of their ancestors. His brother Joe had a beautiful tenor voice, Sarah a mellow alto, and Jake a baritone. They learned to harmonize with his mother's soprano.

One day when they attended their regular Amish church service the congregation sang a German song that begged for some harmony. So, Jake, Joe, and Sarah added harmony which created an outcry from the ministers. They came later to have a talk with Jake's family saying that singing harmony in a church service was "verboten".

The German songs from the Ausbund all sounded somewhat like Gregorian chants and could only be sung in unison. Harmony was simply not allowed. From then on, they never harmonized again in the Amish church service.

This incident reminded Jake of his mother's story about when she was in early grade school. Her teachers had her skip a grade because of her advanced learning skills. She and two of her sisters were known for their harmony singing. They were asked to perform for a local radio station. They had to decline because the Amish church did not approve of that. His mother then had to leave school after fourth grade to help with the work on the farm and eventually became well known as an accomplished seamstress.

After his senior year in high school Jake was asked to be the second tenor in a Mennonite male quartet that toured the Midwest Mennonite churches. This was Jake's first venture into a house of worship. The Amish held their services at the home of members on every two-week rotation. On the tour most of the performances were held inside, but one time it was outdoors. The quartet was singing a song about the blood of Jesus when a fly landed on the music page. Jake meant to swat the fly away but accidentally killed the bloody fly on the page by the word blood. The quartet could barely suppress their laughter for the next verse.

Whenever Jake sang, he sorely missed his brother Joe whose voice was stilled forever after he was killed in the car-buggy accident. Joe had an exceptionally beautiful first tenor voice. He had taught Jake some of the Swiss yodeling songs, but his favorite that stayed with him was "Chime Bells are Ringing" with a very complicated yodel.

Many years later he performed this song in a show in Chicago and in his mind, he sang this to his long-gone brother who had also taught Jake how to read shape notes. This system greatly improved Jake's ability to read music since the different shapes indicated whether the note was do, or re, or mi, and so forth. But while he sang in a chorus in college, he had much more difficulty reading music because they didn't use the shape note system. When he asked the director whether they could use music with shape notes he was stunned when the director asked, "What's that?"

The Pennsylvania Dutch Amish, unlike the Swiss Amish, held what they called "Singings", for the young folks after they turned age sixteen. Jake only attended a few of these events and didn't enjoy them. First, they only had a few who would gather to sing and many of them could barely sing on pitch. Secondly, they all spoke Pennsylvania Dutch, so Jake had difficulty understanding them since his family spoke a Swiss German dialect or English. Jake never became proficient in their language.

These gatherings seemed to exist primarily for beer drinking and sexual activities, the period often referred to as "Rumspringa" time that occurred from age sixteen to the time they married, usually by age nineteen or twenty. This was the time to sow one's wild oats and some of the boys didn't dress Amish and even owned cars. When they got married, they returned to their Amish ways. It seemed to Jake that the boys who were the wildest transgressors of the Amish way of life often became the staunchest and strictest Amish once they returned.

5

Letters from Home

Periodically Jake would get a letter from his mother. This was the only way she had to stay in touch since Amish were not allowed telephones. Of course, radios and electricity were also forbidden. Her letters expressed how much she missed him but once she had crossed out the name Joe and replaced it with his name.

She gave him the latest news about the farm crops and that his father had to retain an Amish farmhand to help him with the farming. He had to sell some of his Brown Swiss milkers since he was left alone with all the milking. Jake felt bad about not being there to help and sad about how lonely his mother sounded. Even though he felt guilty he knew there was no way he could ever go back to the Amish way of life, but he couldn't say that to his mother.

In a later letter his mother wrote about the death of Erv, his Amish childhood playmate. Jake had known Erv since he was eight years old. They used to play tag, softball, and climb in the haymow. In elementary school they were always competing both in sports and in the classroom trying to see who could get the highest grades.

Jake was shocked about the news of the death because Erv was only twenty-one, had just married an Amish girl, {a common age for Amish boys to get married} and had just started his own business of building single and double buggies for the Amish. The obituary said he died suddenly of arteriosclerotic heart disease. The autopsy also revealed that he was born with only one kidney.

Jake assumed Erv might not ever have seen a medical doctor just like himself. The Amish tended to see doctors for only the most serious illnesses and accidents like broken arms or legs. That night Jake cried himself to sleep filled with sadness about forever losing his friend. This sadness then triggered off the other losses of his life. The loss of his first girlfriend, Ellie was a painful memory and the horrible memory of losing his admired brother. It felt like the powerful merging of two rivers creating a super delta. It was a long night.

The next morning Bill asked Jake, "Is everything okay with you? I woke up a bit last night and I thought I heard you crying." "Yeah, I'm okay now, sorry I bothered you," was all he said. He didn't ever disclose to his roommate the story of his friend dying or of his brother's death. He kept his distance.

But that day Jake had a three-hour break between classes, so he found a small semi soundproof room with a piano in the music building. Playing piano by ear and singing the Swiss songs of his childhood was the primary way he used to soothe his sadness. His brother Joe who was very gifted musically had taught him the basic chord structure he could use on the piano.

When he was nine years old his father, Amos, was told by an "English" neighbor that he could have their piano for the price of moving it. With tears streaming down her cheeks, his mother said, "We can't do that, Amish don't allow musical instruments."

Jake overheard Joe asking mother, Mary, "But don't you believe in the Bible?" "Of course," she replied. "It's God's Holy Word." "Well then," he said. "Don't you know Psalms 150 instructs us to use musical instruments?" His mother was dumbfounded. She had the mistaken idea that Amish rules called "ordnung" were all Scripture based. Finally, she relented and as a compromise they agreed to put the piano in the buggy shed. They covered the piano with a big tan horse blanket to hide it from Amish neighbors so they wouldn't be offended.

So, in that buggy shed is where Jake taught himself to play the piano by ear. In the wintertime he had to wear gloves with the fingertips cut off to practice and he had to ignore a few of the keys that were not in tune.

6

Education

Jake loved his college courses. Each one opened a whole new world to him. But he was always nervous at the beginning of each course since the syllabi handed out by the professors were so extensive it seemed to Jake each professor acted as if his was the only course students were taking. Jake found this very intimidating.

He was very competitive and perfectionistic. Even though he did well in all his classes, he was screwed coming and going. If he earned any grade less than an A, he felt like a failure. If he got an A, he assumed that the course was too easy. This perfectionistic trait created many sleepless nights. His primary competitiveness came from inside his head that held an unreachable ideal, his talented dead brother, Joe. Jake often said to himself, "I'm doing the best I can, Joe."

He also carried inside a deeply felt insecurity about having a poor grade school beginning. He was sent to a one-room schoolhouse, grades one through eight, where all the students were Amish. The only non-Amish was the lady teacher who was very hard of hearing. One day a boy was playing with a balloon that burst and the teacher didn't even hear it.

At this school Jake was teased by the other Amish boys for always getting good grades. One boy even said, "Checky, don't you know school's not gonna help us learn how to farm with horses. We're outta here by age sixteen if not before."

Jake also remembered the time in first grade when he accidentally dropped a special red pencil, his mother had given him, into the human feces in the school's outhouse. He had cried when he realized there was no way to retrieve the pencil and cringed about having to tell his mother.

Sitting in his European history class felt like a century had passed since that time. In many ways Jake's early life on the Amish farm was akin to the general population of a century ago.

Jake threw himself into the study of the development of authoritarianism of both Hitler and Stalin and their effective use of propaganda to solidify their political power. One of the primary struggles for Jake was trying to understand the concept of the hook and eye in relationship to the phenomenon of authoritarianism.

Amish at one time discouraged the use of buttons but promoted the use of the hook and eye. If there is a hook, there must be an eye for a connection to be made. So, if there is an autocratic leader, the hook, there must be the eye of people either consciously or unconsciously complying.

It reminded Jake of the time his father said, "We can all be fooled sometimes by a conman." Jake began to realize how Hitler hooked into the antisemitism, resentments, and hate of the German populace to support his platform. Hitler became the supreme conman hook.

This reminded Jake of the milder form of authoritarianism of the Amish Bishop, whose arrogance was fueled by ignorance while appearing humble. Jake was convinced that ignorance breeds arrogance.

He remembered the time the bishop, who was very rule bound, used his power to excommunicate his father for borrowing an English neighbor's tractor to plow a ten-acre field. Spring rains came late that year, and it was already June. His father was desperate to finish the planting and he could plow the field in less than a day if he used a tractor. It would've taken most of a week with the plow horses. Mother insisted he make a full confession to the whole congregation so he could be reinstated to the church and not end up going to hell.

The course in Political Science was another completely foreign subject, and eyeopener for Jake. As an Amish boy his family didn't have newspapers or radio to learn news of the world or politics. Jake wasn't even sure if his mother knew the name of president Eisenhour. He was impressed how the other students in class knew their senators' names and what they stood for. Some even knew how to contact their congressmen.

However, Jake enjoyed the Sun and Moon theories about the waxing and waning of American political parties. This was new to him and reminded him how the Amish weren't even supposed to vote in the elections. He was certain his father was aware of some political news because he sometimes referred to politicians as babbling brooks.

One day when Jake was still home on the farm, his mother was upset that after his father had seen a doctor for his back, he came home with a magazine from the waiting room to read. He liked to read. Although they only had a few books at home like *The Robe* which Jake gave his father one Christmas, and the *Martyrs Mirror* and the Bible in German. Jake's brother Joe had taught him how to read the German Bible.

While Jake's boundless curiosity got him to enjoy all his classes, except math, his primary driving interest that developed was the study of psychology, abnormal psychology, and personality theorists. This intellectual pursuit involved analytic thinking that seemed like a century removed from the simplistic Amish mentality of thinking in black and white or right or wrong conceptualization. He felt certain he had discovered more about who he was becoming. He delved into Freud, Jung, Erickson, Adler, and Maslow, among others, but his deepest attraction veered toward Freud's psychoanalysis. Jung worried him once he detected that Jung experienced a psychotic break in his late thirties. Freud's emphasis on the unconscious was most appealing since it seemed to dovetail into Jake's own experience of always trying to decipher the meaning behind words that often covered up the speaker's true feelings. This intellectual pursuit seemed to make it more difficult for Jake to leave college and return to his Amish home, even for the summer break.

7

Home for the Summer

Jake's scholarship didn't cover all school expenses. He wanted to attend summer school. He wished he didn't have to return to the Amish community, but he needed to make money to cover expenses. So, he worked in a mobile home factory that employed many Amish men. The factory moved into the country to enable it to hire the Amish for their excellent labor and because they did not believe in unionizing.

Jake went home each summer and his mother welcomed him with open arms. Sometimes he felt a bit like the prodigal son who returned to his family after being gone for a long time. His mother made his favorite cherry pie and invited his sister, Sarah, and her three boys over for the event.

Johnny, the ten-year-old, asked intrusive questions. "Uncle Jake, why is your hair so short? It's supposed to be longer. And don't you know you're not supposed to wear colored shirts, and pants with a belt?" Jake just smiled but didn't have any response to his nephew, but he asked, "Want to play some catch, Johnny?" "Yeah," he yelled.

In the summers Jake continued to date Viola. After three years of college Jake was twenty-four and he felt an internal pressure to get married. His girlfriend, Viola, was worried because she had missed her period sometime after they had been intimate. They set a wedding date for August fifth, his mother's birthday.

This was a typical Mennonite wedding held in a church house and Jake wasn't sure if his mother would attend because as an Amish person, she wasn't supposed to enter a house of worship. Her love for her son won out. Besides, his father Amos had insisted they attend.

Jake had desperately prayed that Viola was not pregnant. It turned out to be a false alarm, but he never knew if this was an answered prayer. He was always confused whenever he prayed because he was torn between the image in his head of the judgmental, wrathful God of the Amish or the Mennonite God of Love. He tried very hard to imagine the God of Love, but the memory of his brother's death always interfered. So, most of the times he prayed felt more like sending his thoughts into a huge empty ether.

From his readings on religion and philosophy he became aware that belief in God appeared to be a universal phenomenon and that in part all religions existed for the psychological purpose of managing the human anxiety about the "unknown". He often wondered whether God created man or man created God for the purpose of retaining the magical thinking in adulthood of the universal childhood magical thinking that enabled them to believe in Santa Claus. They seemed very similar to Jake.

By the time Jake was a college senior, he finally felt competent and more of a sense of belonging, at least to the college community. He still didn't have close friends but maintained many good acquaintances. His professors liked him and several of them asked Jake to become their TA. He chose the psychology department where he had to pass out exams and sometimes had to grade them, including essay questions with a grading key supplied by the professor.

After graduating with honors, he applied and was accepted at both the University of Columbia, New York, and the University of Chicago. New York scared the daylights out of him, so he chose to attend Chicago, often referred to as the Harvard of the Midwest.

8

Graduate School and Marriage

Jake and Viola got married when Jake was the ripe old age of twenty-four in the Amish tradition and the young age for the English culture. Together they moved to Chicago for graduate school. Jake gradually became more aware that he still couldn't feel very attached, not even to his new wife. But he was shocked when one night she didn't even come home until the next morning. She had started an affair with a fellow student at the community college.

Jake was devastated. He blamed himself for taking his wife for granted partly because there is no such thing as divorce in the Amish. He was so deep into his studies he didn't realize the gulf that had developed between them.

When Jake's sister Sarah heard of the marriage difficulties, she used a pay phone to warn him that divorce would kill their mother. Jake searched the Bible for the Biblical position on divorce. He found so many contradictory messages on this subject that he decided to listen to his own heart, so he could be at peace with himself. He realized the devastation he felt about divorcing his wife was more about not disappointing his mother than the pain of losing Viola.

9

Psychoanalysis

After getting his divorce and his doctorate at the same time, Jake wanted to pursue the study of psychoanalysis. He was determined. Jake was aware of his non-compliant personality trait. Since the Amish were so rule-bound he found himself balking like a horse against many of the rules like how he got his hair cut. This non-compliance stayed with him for the rest of his life. Even the heavy Amish blanket meant to squelch curiosity never succeeded with him. He was bursting with hunger for education and learning.

After receiving his doctorate, he wanted to pursue more training in psychoanalysis when he discovered the Psychoanalytic institute had a rule that their program accepted only M.D.s. Jake said to himself, watch me. He proceeded to contact an internationally famous Psychoanalyst and proposed a private training and paying whatever he needed. This proposal was accepted and advanced training in psychoanalysis continued for a number of years.

He came to regard the Institute filled with members as the educated Amish with their rules and followerism. Early on even Freud wrote a scathing letter denouncing the limiting of training only for medical doctors. In 1926 he vigorously defended the training of non-MDs for psychoanalysis.

Jake hung out his own shingle on Michigan Avenue where he started his own private practice. The work was draining and difficult, but he also found it gratifying. In the course of a psychoanalysis the dynamics often shift with the patient moving from a positive transference state to a negative one. Jake chuckled to himself with the thought he used to pitch manure with a pitchfork, now he's hauling shit symbolically. The more things change the more they stay the same. Well, perhaps not. He fell deeply in love for the first time.

He had experienced a seismic shift inside from his personal analysis that allowed him to feel an empathic attachment to someone other than his mother. His consultant had referred him to an experienced psychoanalyst. When he went in for his first appointment he said, "Doctor, unbeknownst to you I have been having sessions with you for a year." The analyst replied, "In that case lie down on the couch and continue talking to me." So began his four times per week analysis.

Jake described his insomnia. "I'm scared to go to sleep. Every night I have horrible dreams of dangerous snakes trying to bite me. I struggle and struggle to get away but can't move. Then wake up with a sweat. So, I get up and practice my Gibson guitar and sing the old Swiss songs quietly. I finally fall asleep toward morning."

Once Jake became aware of his fear of his own aggression and was able to accept it and even embrace it, his insomnia disappeared. But he still kept practicing his Gibson, just not so late at night.

Sometimes strange things happened in analysis. During one session lying on the couch his back got extremely hot. He said to the Doctor, "I may have to sit up because my back feels like it's burning up." "Okay," the doctor said. "But just try and stay with the moment and we'll see what comes up." That's when Jake remembered the story of his birth his mother told him. He was born in the Amish home. He was born so prematurely that he only weighed three pounds. One of his aunts served as a midwife. When the doctor finally arrived, he examined the baby boy and declared to the aunt that they better plan for a funeral because the baby would not survive.

His mother responded to this information by heating bricks on top of the wood burning stove. Once they were heated, she wrapped them with blankets and placed the infant on top. She had created a homemade incubator. The baby survived and thrived, bypassing the need for a funeral. Of course, Jake's mother believed God must have chosen the baby for something special.

By the time Jake finished relating this story the heat on his back had dissipated. He wondered if this was the phenomenon referred to as muscle memory.

One time after leaving a session he ran into a colleague, a woman, who invited him to a party at her Hyde Park apartment. He knew this would be a typical Hyde Park party with smoking, drinking and dancing to the Supremes. He was glad he had learned how to dance.

During a snowstorm in 1967 in Chicago, a lady friend had invited him to her apartment so she could teach him how to dance to the Motown sound. The snow was so deep there was no traffic on the streets. He walked to her place in the middle of the street. His friend invited him in and that's where he learned to dance.

When Jake got to the party his colleague welcomed him and introduced him to Darlene, her roommate. As the party progressed, he noticed that Darlene was there with a boyfriend, but he couldn't keep his eyes off her. She was a beautiful brunette who was a good dancer and wore the sexiest polka-dot bell bottoms he had ever seen. Once he got the nerve to ask her to dance, she was genuinely friendly. During the dance he thought she looked like a combination of a young Sophia Loren and Shirley MacLaine. He fell. Hard.

For the next six months he debated about whether he should call her since she was at the party with a boyfriend. When he finally called her for a date, he was afraid she might not even remember who he was. He was surprised that not only did she remember him but said, "I'd love to go on a date with you." That was the beginning of a wonderful romance.

When they got married Jake was dumbfounded that his Amish parents came to the wedding in Bond Chapel since the

Amish don't allow divorce or remarriage. That day was a wonderful day for Jake to marry the beautiful Darlene and with the inherent blessings of his father and mother. He never felt more loved than on that day.

Jake became aware that in this marriage he was able to feel a deep empathic attachment with his wife reminiscent of his love for his mother. After several years they had a beautiful baby boy. Three years later they also had a sweet baby girl. His feelings for the children were so deep he now knew that he was even capable of killing anyone who would seriously threaten them.

10

Case Vignettes

Jake's private practice continued to thrive in his Michigan Avenue office. The work was challenging but also gratifying. A medical doctor had referred a new patient, a woman, to him because after giving her a thorough neurological examination, he couldn't detect anything wrong. The lady had difficulty walking without a cane.

She walked in with the cane for her first analytic appointment. She was an attractive woman, well dressed with beautiful black hair. Jake began the session by asking, "What is your take on why your doctor referred you to me?" She looked up and said with a smirk, "Oh, my doctor thinks my problem is in my head. But it's not in my head. It's in my damn legs."

"Okay," Jake said. "Maybe we could start by having you tell me something about your family." Jake learned to pay close attention to the narrative. Would she first begin with her father or her mother? She soon opened up and told the story about how she was the third child with two older brothers in a Westside

Italian mafia family. Her father had a huge temper and as a little girl she overheard him yelling about offing people. Later she learned that meant killing people. She often went to bed frightened out of her wits and frequently woke up with violent dreams.

As is often the pattern, for the first many sessions this patient developed a strong positive transference toward the therapist. But Jake knew in time the other shoe would drop, that is, the negative transference would develop. She became increasingly angry and even belligerent toward the therapist until one day she stood up from the couch and yelled at him, "You're nothing but a God-damned quack. My legs still don't work right." As she stormed out of the office she yelled, "And I'm not coming back."

Jake noticed she had forgotten to take her cane with her. Two days later she called and with a sheepish sounding voice said she would like to make another appointment. When she came in, she explained she was so enraged after the last session and practically ran to her car. When she arrived home, she realized she forgot her cane and marveled how well her legs functioned. Since that incident she has had no trouble with her legs.

It became clear to Jake that the patient had made the difficult adaptation of expressing her fear of her rage by psychologically creating dysfunctional legs where she could neither fight nor flee. After a number of additional sessions, she ended treatment with excellent results.

Another patient, a Mr. Y, was referred by a former patient. He owned an engineering firm that employed thirty engineers. He was a tall handsome man in his forties with jet black hair.

When Jake asked, "So what brings you to analysis?" Mr. Y explained that he was told he has an anger problem. "How does your anger manifest itself?" Jake asked. He then described how last week he got so angry at a defective typewriter; he threw it across his office.

Taking his history revealed that when Mr. Y was thirteen years old his father had come into his room to talk to him and had promptly fallen on his bed and died immediately of a heart attack. Mr. Y could not recall any of his emotions from that event except that he remembered being shocked. Further analysis revealed this horrendous event laid the foundation for the compulsive repetitive response of explosive anger to any experiences of disappointments. This repetitive response was the observable behavior, but what remained unconscious were the powerful emotions that stemmed from the event of his father dying on his bed.

Jake had learned that if we don't remember the past, we are bound to repeat it. He knew this was true for organizations and government, but it was even more true for each individual person. So, it was his job as the analyst to decipher the unconscious repetitional pattern of each patient. The repetitional pattern may be positive or negative, but, of course, the focus is primarily on the negative since that is what brings a patient in for treatment.

During the four years of treatment Mr. Y frequently experienced disappointments that then enraged him. But the most useful analytic tool for helping him gradually become aware of his repetition happened when the analyst was the source of disappointment. For example, Mr. Y threatened to leave treatment saying he didn't feel respected. Jake scoured his own self trying to find out how he might have disappointed him. Then Jake discovered that he had made a mistake in the billing. Mr. Y admitted that was what enraged him and made him feel disrespected. Experiences like this helped him develop an awareness of his previously unconscious repetition.

Eight months later Jake commented to Mr. Y, "It seems to me that together we have accomplished why you first came to see me. Why are you still here? I also noticed you keep bringing personnel matters for us to discuss." To Jake's surprise, Mr. Y explained, "This process makes me too much money to quit. You see, I'm learning to empathically listen to my employees. Instead of flying off the handle and firing them, I try to help solve their problems. So, the absentee and turnover rates have drastically reduced, the two items that are very expensive for a business. That's how this makes me money."

11

Jake's Family

The highlight of Jake's day was going home from work to be with his wife, Darlene, and his son and daughter, Johnny and Jilly. His wife regaled him with stories about their kids' experiences while he was at work. One time when Johnny was three years old, he had a playdate with a little neighborhood girl his age. Darlene overheard the little girl saying to Johnny, "When we get older you and I could get married." Johnny replied, "Why would I get married, I already have a mother." This gave Jake a chuckle as he thought, and his son hadn't yet even read Freud.

One day after getting home from work, Jake sat on the lawn chair in his front yard. Jilly, then age six, wearing a pretty pink dress, brought her little chair over and sat beside him. "Well, daddy, how was your day?" Jake said, "It was good. What's on your mind?" "Ya know daddy, I was thinking that when I get bigger, I'm gonna get married and have six babies. "Wow," he said, "that would be a big family. How would you take care of that many kids?" "Oh," she replied, "I'd get you to help me. Gotta go play now," she said as she dashed off to the neighbors.

Jake delighted in his children's normal psychological development which was such a stark contrast to his work in abnormal psychology. The contrast from being with paranoid patients to being with his trusting kids. From his kids' developmental issues to his patients' negative repetitions stemming from damaging traumatic experiences. But it was clear to Jake that an effective psychoanalysis is never about blaming the parents. It is about trying to help patients take ownership for what they create based on their past experiences, to learn how they are unknowingly repeating their past. It is amazing to what extent we help create what we end up experiencing.

Two men caught in a traffic jam, one, for historical reasons, creates a road rage experience. The other man accepts what he can't control and listens to Mozart for his experience of the same external event.

12

Case Vignette

Jake had also developed a reputation for successfully treating suicidal patients. A young woman, Ms. X, a psychologist, was referred to Jake by a physician. She was an attractive lady with dark hair and complexion. She worked in a hospital department administering psychological tests for children.

When she came in for her first appointment, Jake noticed her eyes had a suspicious, untrusting look. Her history revealed she was sexually abused by an uncle when she was only five years old. After a number of sessions, she thanked Jake for not trying to shake hands with her at the first appointment. She explained ever since her abuse she was somehow able to numb her hands to avoid feeling the touch of any stranger's hands.

Ms. X seemed able to keep her paranoia in check enough at her job of testing. But as her treatment progressed her paranoia was increasingly evidenced in her analytic sessions. In one appointment she stood by the door, refused to enter the office then blurted out, "Why did you hit me in the back when I left the last time I was here?" Jake merely asked, "Why would I do that?" She was still sitting on the couch musing the question. Then she looked at Jake and with a surprised, quizzical look said, "OH, you didn't hit me, did you?" Jake nodded no. Then she laid down on the couch and the session proceeded.

More history revealed that she had grown up with a mother who was diagnosed as a paranoid schizophrenic. Her brother wouldn't have anything to do with the mother. So, Ms. X was alone as the caretaker for the mother who was institutionalized for many years. She would make weekly visits to her mother who didn't seem to even appreciate her daughter's efforts.

Jake was concerned about the implications of the patient's over identification with the mother. He was afraid her current functioning was based on the thin thread that depended on the mother being alive to provide a differentiation of her and her mother. The place of the me, not me. When she visited her mother, she experienced the paranoia as belonging to her mother, not herself.

After ten years of treatment that enabled Ms. X to function in her job, she was fired at the same time that her mother died. These two coinciding events were extremely devastating. No matter what Jake did or tried to intervene made any difference. She rapidly deteriorated and became more and more like her deceased mother.

She only wanted to talk about how suicide was the only solution. Jake reluctantly accepted the fact that once a person has made the decision to commit suicide, there was nothing anybody could do to prevent that. Jake had already learned the primary difference between homicide and suicide was where the gun was pointed. They both were expressions of murderous rage combined with extreme hopelessness in the suicidal person. It was a difficult time for Jake when the call came from her brother that his sister was found hanging by a rope in her house.

13

Sad News

Not long after that bad news, Jake's sister Sarah called him from a pay phone informing him that their mother was in a hospital. Jake called the attending physician. He was told that his mother had an inoperable colon cancer.

Jake immediately cancelled all appointments for the next two weeks and made arrangements for his family to make the trip home. When they arrived at the old home place his father came out to the car to greet them. Jake promptly hugged his father, one of the few times they had ever hugged. His father seemed a bit uncomfortable. He didn't cry, just looked very sad.

He and Sarah had moved mother from the hospital to a hospital bed set up in the living room. Mother insisted on getting up from the bed to help Sarah make Jake's last favorite cherry pie. That was the best cherry pie Jake ever ate for the rest of his life.

Later that night, while writhing in pain, mother asked Sarah and Jake to sing her favorite Swiss German songs. She especially requested, "In Dem Himmel ist Ruh." {In Heaven there is rest} She knew she was dying.

Jake went out onto the back porch for a breather. There was a full moon to the southwest. As he looked up at the moon he was flooded with long forgotten memories. When Jake was only three his mother took him to her father's funeral. There were many Amish people all dressed in black standing around the freshly dug grave that held the pine casket for his grandfather. Jake's curiosity got him to walk to the edge of the pit to look at the coffin when his mother roughly grabbed his arm, pulled him back and said, "You could fall in there."

When he was four years old Jake and his mother traveled by bus to the Berne, Indiana area to visit her mother who lived with her youngest son John. It was an Amish tradition for the youngest son to take over the parent's homestead. The bus dropped them off on a gravel road. It was already dark when they had to walk the mile to John's farm. The moon was out but it cast eerie shadows, especially by the movement of the cows and horses across the fence. That was when Jake was astounded to discover that his strong, competent mother felt afraid for she held his hand too tight for too long.

When Jake went back inside, his mother asked him to hold her hand. His father was nodding off in his chair and Sarah was in the kitchen. His wife had put the kids to bed and stayed upstairs with them. Mother started to talk about how she hoped Jesus would welcome her to heaven. "You know," she said, "That's all we Amish can do, is to just hope. We can't say we're saved like some of those English people do. We can only hope." She added, "Sure hope I'll get to see your brother Joe."

Jake still didn't cry out loud, but tears began to fill his eyes as he tried to reassure her. "Surely Jesus must want to welcome you. You've been such a wonderful mother."

That night after saying good night to his mother he stayed up for a long time. He couldn't go to sleep. His memories kept him awake. He remembered the story his mother told him about the doctor saying she should plan for a funeral, that Jake as a preemie wouldn't survive.

She also often repeated the story about the time the family had gone to someone's house for church services. It was summertime and she had let Jake out of her sight. He was only a little over a year old and still in diapers. He had crawled onto the slanted doors leading to the basement. The doors must have given way because someone noticed a baby floating on his back in the water filled basement. His mother always added that God saved him twice, so, He might have a special purpose for Jake.

He also remembered one of her favorite jokes. When they had visitors, she liked to ask, "How do they call potatoes in Germany?" While they were struggling for the German word for potatoes she would explain, "They don't call them, they dig them just like we do." She'd howl with laughter amidst the response of groans.

Finally, Jake was falling asleep when he relived the times when he was little, and he would protest his mother trying to get him to take a nap. When she picked him up to rock him, he would plead, "Don't sing 'By Oh Baby'," because he knew her singing would promptly put him to sleep.

The next morning, she died in her sleep. His father was already up, clothed in his stoicism. All he said was, "As we all know death is just a part of life," reminiscent of what he said when Jake's dog Frisky was shot because he was too old to survive another winter.

14

The Funeral

Mary's body was taken immediately for embalming by Yoder/Culp funeral home where the viewing of the body was scheduled four days later in the week. The viewing room was a large space that could readily hold one hundred fifty people. Many Amish people, a mixture of Pennsylvania Dutch and Swiss Amish, arrived at the funeral home driven by hired non-Amish drivers. A few locals drove up in their horse and buggies by the hitching posts.

Jake's mother came from a large family of fifteen, so most of her immediate family came to the viewing. This included many of Jake's first cousins he had only met a few times. The men wore black barndoor trousers held up by suspenders and white or light blue shirts.

They wore unkempt beards for their church didn't allow them to trim them or allow them to have a mustache. This tradition of not allowing a mustache began in the eighteen hundreds to differentiate them from the military and fashion of the time.

Some of the men cousins reeked of cigarette smoke. They stayed crowded together in a group and at times Jake caught several of them looking askance at him and his family.

Jake became very agitated when he watched his mother's sisters, all in black dresses and white head coverings, hovering around the casket wailing and bawling as they viewed the body. Jake imagined they were thinking how his mother couldn't possibly go to heaven since she didn't follow all rules of their church. Jake kept thinking, "Sure, now you can show your respects, now that she is dead, but when she was alive you shunned her."

Jake whispered to his wife and kids, "I gotta get outta here for a breather. Going for a walk." His wife guessed why he had to leave. But his son, Johnny, who was now fourteen, and very intuitive asked, "Where are you going, Dad?" Jake said, "I'll be back soon." His daughter, Jilly, just gave him a hug.

On his walk Jake wondered how his father was able to tolerate the scene the sisters were creating. He guessed that his father's stoic nature probably came in handy for times like this.

After the burial Jake's deep sadness and sense of profound loss was beyond words to describe. He wished he could be alone in the woods of his childhood and let his sadness take its painful course. The loss of his beloved mother triggered and evoked all the losses he had experienced throughout his life. He relived the terrible loss of his admired brother Joe. The loss of Ellie, his girlfriend at age sixteen, who wrote that she loved him too much to continue. The loss of his boyhood friend, Erv, to a heart attack when he was only twenty. The loss of his first wife, Viola, from a divorce. And finally, the loss of his dog, Frisky, who was shot because he was too old to survive another winter.

Jake was in such deep mourning he even lost for a time the memory of spending time with his father after the burial. Jake had to cancel all patient appointments for another two weeks before he felt ready to again meet the challenge of treating difficult patients.